TEN
OWIES

By Tony Johnston

Pictures by
Annabel Tempest

GREENWILLOW BOOKS
An Imprint of HarperCollinsPublishers

FOR MY GRANDCHILDREN,
WITH THEIR ENDLESS OWIES—NOAH, YANNIK,
MALLELAI, SORAYA, AND LADAAN—T. J.

FOR MY NIECE, LITTLE CHLOE,
WHO IS ALWAYS COVERED
IN OWIES, AS SHE IS SO INTREPID!—A. T.

Ten Owies. Text copyright © 2022 by Tony Johnston. Illustrations copyright © 2022 by Annabel Tempest
All rights reserved. Manufactured in Italy.
For information address HarperCollins Children's Books, a division of HarperCollins Publishers, 195 Broadway,
New York, NY 10007. www.harpercollinschildrens.com
The art was created digitally in Adobe™Photoshop™ with pencil, paper, scanned handmade textures.

Library of Congress Cataloging-in-Publication Data is available. ISBN 978-0-06-264460-2 (hardcover)

First Edition 22 23 24 25 26 RTLO 10 9 8 7 6 5 4 3 2 1   Greenwillow Books

Olivia loved ice cream.
Most any kind you please.

She gobbled up a bowlful.

Oh, yikes!

A big brain freeze.

ONE OWIE.

Alberto, on the top bunk,
was jouncing on the bed.

He boinged up to the ceiling
and bonked and wonked his head.

TWO OWIES.

Delilah climbed a maple
to see what she could see.

But she fell down—quite quickly—
and cronkled up her knee.

THREE OWIES.

Young Thomas stuffed his footsie into his mouth. Oh, no!

By accident, he chomped down
and bit his baby toe.

FOUR OWIES.

Anita picked
some posies.

She picked
a pink sweet pea.

She chose a rose

and—uh-oh—

got stingered by a bee.

FIVE OWIES.

Maurice enjoyed ice skating,

where wind
just whoops

and blows.

He once tossed off his muffler

and froze

his little nose.

SIX OWIES.

Jazelle could bike like crazy.

Like lightning is the truth.

One day she zoomed her fastest

and crashed and bashed her tooth.

SEVEN OWIES.

Dear Sammy poked a parrot,
a naughtiness for true.

The parrot pecked his finger
all purple, black, and blue.

EIGHT OWIES.

A girl named Mallelita
could pogo-stick like mad.

She spronged into a cactus.

How prickly! How sad!

NINE OWIES.

Once Yulie took a boiled egg
and cracked it on his head.
A bump lumped up like magic.
He wobbled back to bed.

TEN OWIES.

Then daddies kissed the owies.

And mommies sang a song.

Cavort, ca-snort,

and yodel!

The owies are—

ALL

GONE!